..ONSTERS
ARE AFRAID OF
BABIES

WRITTEN BY NICHOLAS TANA

ILLUSTRATED BY
ELISE LEUTWYLER & JESSICA ABBOTT

COPYRIGHT 2019 BY NEW CLASSICS BOOKS LLC

NEW CLASSICS

MONSTERS ARE AFRAID OF BABIES!

THE WAY THEY LOOK...

ARRRGGGG...

THE WAY
THEY CRY...

BBBLLAAAARRGG

THE WAY THEY SMELL...

IT'S NO WONDER WHY...

EEWWWW

BABIES MAKE MONSTERS WANT TO CRY!

IT'S THE WAY THEY

CREEP AROUND...

TURN THINGS INSIDE OUT...

AND UPSIDE DOWN...

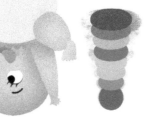

SO IF YOU FIND YOU'RE AFRAID OF MONSTERS...

BECAUSE THEY ARE SPOOKY AND SCARY...

STICKY AND
ICKY...

CRAZY AND CREEPY...

LOUD AND STINKY...

JUST REMEMBER
WHAT TO DO...

KEEP A **BABY** CLOSE TO YOU!

DEDICATED TO AND INSPIRED BY

PAOLO & LUCIA

- THE AUTHOR

RIC, SUE, KIM & COLE

LUCAS & LESLEE

- THE ILLUSTRATORS

CHOO CHOOOOOOOOO

CPSIA information can be obtained
at www.ICGtesting.com
Printed in the USA
LVHW072112291220
675337LV00014B/299